STARTING OUT

HELICOPTERS

MEG GREVE

CREATIVE EDUCATION • CREATIVE PAPERBACKS

CONT

ENTS

I SEE A HELICOPTER.

Blades whirl.

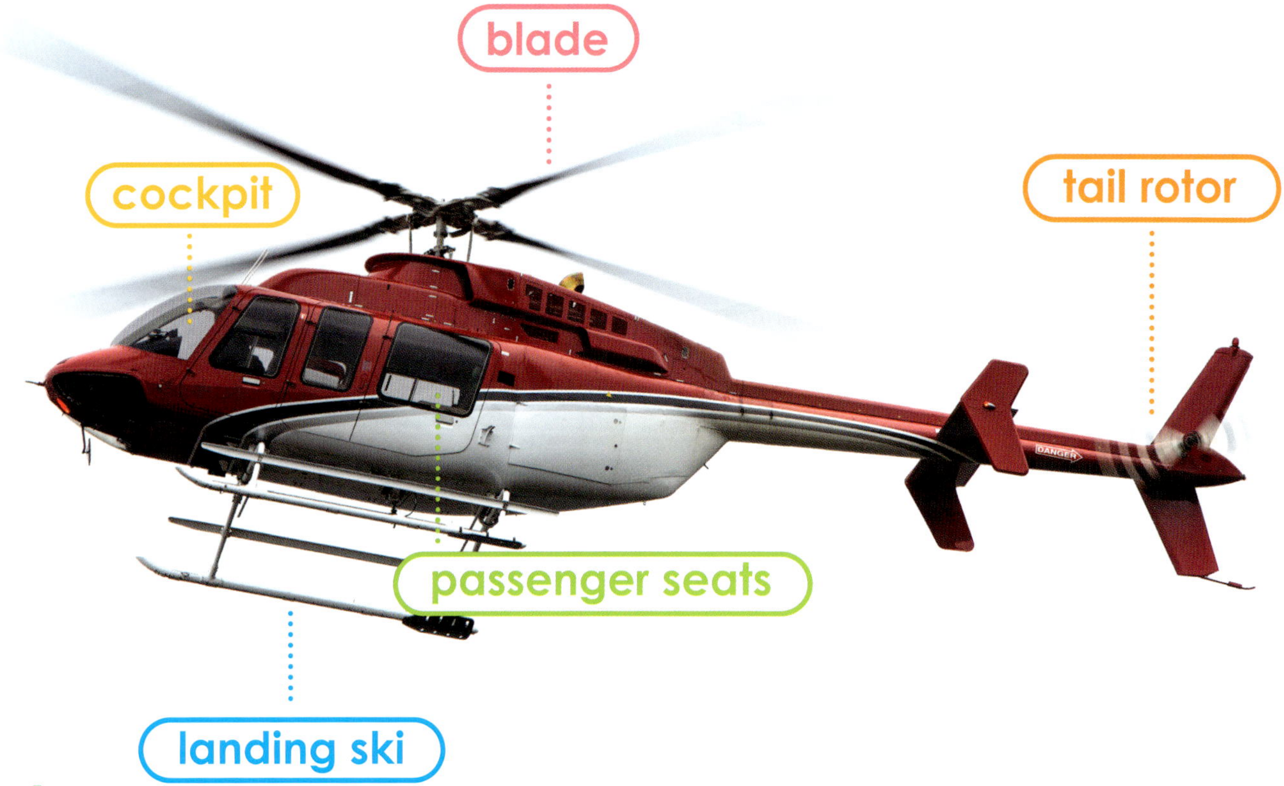

It takes off straight up into the air.

I think a helicopter flies like a dragonfly.

The blades spin like a fan.

A helicopter is different than a plane. A helicopter can **hover** over one spot. It can fly low.

I imagine I am a helicopter

pilot. I land in small spaces.

I rescue people in trouble.

I fly in all directions!

Helicopters help put out fires.

Helicopters can hover over volcanoes.
A helicopter may be used to explore Mars!

Where will I go someday in a helicopter?

MAKE A NOISE

PPA, CHOPPA!

Can you make the sounds of a helicopter?

Listen to these sounds:

https://www.youtube.com/watch?v=e8BAckZBQZc

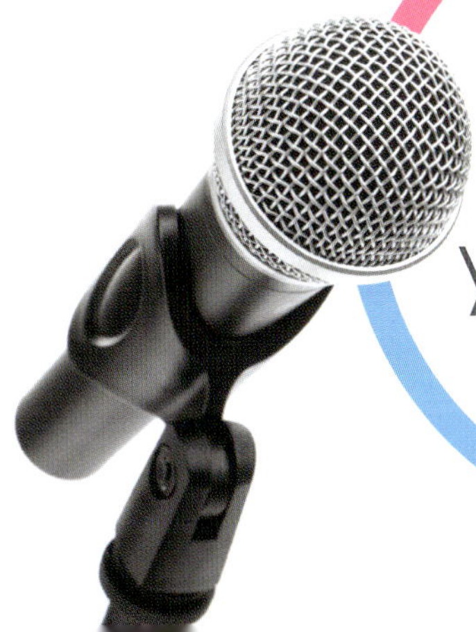

Now it is your turn!

HELICOPTER WORDS

blades: the parts on a helicopter that spin so it can fly

hover: to stay over one spot

pilot: a person who flies a helicopter or an airplane

rescue: to save from danger

READING CORNER

Albert, Rosalyn. *Let's Go on a Helicopter*. London: New Frontier Publishing, 2022.

Brody, Walt. *How Military Helicopters Work*. Minneapolis, Minn.: Lerner Publications, 2019.

Read With You Center for Excellence in STEAM Education. *Henry the Helicopter*. Chicago, Ill.: Read With You Publishing, 2022.

INDEX

PUBLISHED BY CREATIVE EDUCATION AND CREATIVE PAPERBACKS
P.O. Box 227, Mankato, Minnesota 56002
Creative Education and Creative Paperbacks are imprints of The Creative Company
www.thecreativecompany.us

LIBRARY OF CONGRESS CATALOGING-IN-PUBLICATION DATA
Names: Greve, Meg, author.
Title: Helicopters / by Meg Greve.
Description: Mankato, Minnesota : Creative Education and Creative Paperbacks, [2025] | Series: Starting out | Includes bibliographical references and index. | Audience: Ages 4-7 | Audience: Grades K-1 | Summary: "Helicopters will introduce budding book learners to a noisy, colorful world with this new Starting Out title. Colorful photos labeled diagrams, 'Make a Noise' section, glossary, and more ignite a passion for learning"--Provided by publisher.
Identifiers: LCCN 2023059459 (print) | LCCN 2023059460 (ebook) | ISBN 9798889891758 (library binding) | ISBN 9781682775608 (paperback) | ISBN 9798889891871 (ebook)
Subjects: LCSH: Helicopters--Juvenile literature. | CYAC: Helicopters. | LCGFT: Instructional and educational works.
Classification: LCC TL716.2 .G74 2025 (print) | LCC TL716.2 (ebook) | DDC 629.133/352--dc23/eng/20240128
LC record available at https://lccn.loc.gov/2023059459
LC ebook record available at https://lccn.loc.gov/2023059460

DESIGN AND PRODUCTION
Design by Rhea Magaro
Production by Beeline Media and Design
Art direction by Tom Morgan
Printed in the United States of America

PHOTOGRAPHS by Alamy (Keith Levit/First Light), Dreamstime (Paul Prescott), Getty Images (dan_prat, 1001Love, Spondylolithesis, Alex Ratson), Shutterstock (EB Adventure Photography, freestore 839, Hintau Aliaksei, kirill_makarov, FCG, Paleka, Photos SS, Bohbeh, Monika Wisniewska)